T0354441

George's Pup

Written by **Dyan Beyer**

Illustrated by **Brianalise Marie**

Romans 12:21:

Do not be overcome by evil. Overcome evil with good!

To order additional copies of this book, contact:
Xlibris
844-714-8691
www.Xlibris.com
Orders@Xlibris.com

ISBN: Softcover   979-8-3694-2064-5
        Hardcover   979-8-3694-2065-2
        EBook   979-8-3694-2063-8

Print information available on the last page

Rev. date: 04/27/2024

This book is dedicated to my 6 grandchildren

George Robert Beyer

Bear Robert Beyer

Grace Mary Beyer

Paul Dolman Beyer

Creed Henry Beyer

Ruth Christine Beyer

Other books by Dyan Beyer

Under Angels' Wings

Baby Boy Bear

Baby Grace Is Here!

Baby Needs Pants

Little Lion

Bear And The Dinosaur

The 5 Wise Grandchildren

One day George was in the park and a pup found him. George played with the pup until it was time to leave. The pup followed George all the way home.

"Pup, you need to go back! You can't come with me. Go on...go home!"
But the dog just wagged his tail and walked into the house along with George!

George told Pup to hide under the kitchen table until he could explain to his mom why a dog was here. Pup stayed quiet for about a minute and then started barking!

"George, what is that dog doing under the kitchen table?" Mom asked.

George explained how Pup followed him home and then he asked if he could keep him. His mom said only if he didn't belong to anyone else and if Dad approved.

They put up lost dog signs around the town. When no one came to claim the dog, Dad said Pup could stay.

George was happy to have his Pup. He fed him and made a bed for the dog to sleep in, "You can sleep here, Pup! Goodnight, see you in the morning!"

As soon as the family went to bed, Pup started to chew on everything he could get his teeth on! Pillows, furniture, toys, you name it, he chewed on it!

Suddenly, a cat appeared. When Pup noticed he was being watched, he stopped and asked her, "Who are you?"

The cat slunk closer, licked her paw and wiped it across her face before answering, "Who am I? I live here! But who are YOU?" She asked pushing her nose against Pup's.

"I'm new here," Pup managed to say.

The cat circled around Pup sizing him up, "A furry INFERIOR CANINE pup who chews up the place!"

"You still didn't tell me who... you are, Cat?" Pup asked backing away.

"Not that I need to answer you but I will. I am the intelligent SUPERIOR four-legged beautiful feline, otherwise known as the QUEEN of the house who, as I said before, lives HERE!"

"Oh...I didn't know all of that!" Pup said cowering down a bit.

"ALONE! No other animals permitted except HIM, who gets on my nerves periodically!" She said pointing to Floyd the parrot. "So tell me again WHO ARE YOU?"

"I'm George's pup..."

"That's what you think. You won't be here long."

"How do you know that?" Pup asked starting to feel sad.

"Because I am the ONLY smart animal around here and there is only room for one four-legged PET in this house. You have to GO especially if you keep chewing up the place!"

4

Pup was a little afraid to speak but then he found the courage to say, "I don't want to go, I like George!"

"Dogs are so sappy! Suit yourself, but stay out of my way!" The cat said.

"I will...hey I'm hungry again. Is there any extra food around here?" Pup asked licking his lips.

The cat gave Pup a once-over look before answering, "I know where the food is but I can never open the bag...if you insist on living here, you can help me. Come on, Pup...is that the name you go by?"

"It is now! Lead the way to the food!"

"Lead the way...lead the way!" Floyd squawked.

Cat tried to tell Pup about behaving by not chewing up the couch pillows but Pup was having too much fun to listen! He chewed all night long on everything he could find!

The next morning when the family came downstairs, the room was a mess!

"What happened? Dad yelled out going over to the sleeping dog.

Mom and George starting picking up the mess while Pup yawned and turned over.

"You did a bad thing, Pup! You can't chew up the pillows and furniture!" Mom said.

Once the mess was cleaned up, George went over to Pup, "You can't ever make that mess again. I'm afraid that if you do, you won't be able to stay here."

Pup licked George's cheek and gave him his paw hoping that he would be forgiven. And he was until the next time he chewed up the house!

Later in the day, Cat found Pup looking very pleased with himself and as happy as can be.

"So I see you are still here. Stupid thing you did by making a complete mess last night! What makes your kind do things such as this?" Cat asked Pup.

"It's a teething thing for me. I can't help it! Do cats not have that problem?" Pup asked.

"You ignorant loud barking creature, cats do not do things that get them kicked out of the house!"

Pup scratched his neck, "Where are you during the day? You seem to disappear."

"Yes I try to keep my distance especially from that bird! And the humans can be just as annoying, always petting me after I groom myself!"

"I like to be petted, most times it takes care of my itching spots!" Pup said.

"ITCHING! Oh please, don't tell me you have fleas!" Cat yelled out.

"Well, I would hope so. Isn't that what all dogs have?"

George and Pup became best friends. George taught Pup how to fetch a ball and do tricks. He taught him the rules of the house. "One, always behave and never lie. Two, always stand up for each other! Three, no more chewing on anything! Do you understand that, Pup?" George asked.

Pup wagged his tail in agreement and all was well until...!

"He did it AGAIN! And that's why our kind is superior." Cat spoke out.

When Mom and Dad woke up to another mess they were not happy! George begged them to give Pup another chance.

"He can't keep chewing on everything! This has got to stop or out you go, Pup!" Dad said.

"Please, Dad, please one last chance, please!" George cried out.

Mom and Dad loved Pup too but there would have to be some changes made.

"We'll give him ONE more chance, George. Maybe a bigger chewing bone will work," Mom said.

Pup and Cat were enjoying eating another one of their midnight snacks. "Try not to chew with your mouth open!" Cat said scolding Pup.

"I'll try but it's not in my nature to do so, Cat."

"Hmm, it seems that you are learning some things from me. Your vocabulary has increased!"

"Why thank you, my furry little friend who is the Queen of the house!" Pup said licking his lips.

"Cut the SARCASM, you are still despicable in every other way, Pup!"

Pup suddenly burped as Cat wiped her mouth on a napkin and added, "And that is why my breed will always be superior!"

"That may be true but without me, Cat, you couldn't have these midnight snacks!"

Cat nodded her head before saying, "At least I do have a purpose for you. I guess you're not so bad."

Cat was the first one up when she realized that Pup went on a chewing spree AGAIN! "Get up! Clean this place up before the owners wake up!" She yelled.

Pup rolled over in his bed and without opening his eyes he said, "I think you are way overthinking this situation Cat..."

It was too late because the family were already down the stairs and staring at the total mess that Pup made! George was the first one to yell out, "NO, NOT AGAIN!"

Mom and Dad told George that Pup would have to go to a family that had a big yard so he could stay outside and not chew on things. George cried but he understood that Pup couldn't stay if he didn't obey.

   "When I come home, George, I'll take him to the Animal Relocation in town." Dad said before leaving for work.

Mom went over to George to give him a hug, "I'm sorry, George, but it's the best thing to do. Come upstairs and get ready for school," Mom said before leaving him alone with Pup.

Pup laid on George's lap. "Why Pup? Why couldn't you stop biting on everything? I'm really going to miss you!"

Pup licked George's tears away and wished he had listened to Cat. Now it was too late. Pup was the saddest dog ever. Once George went upstairs to get dressed, Cat appeared. "So you finally got thrown out! I warned you about your chewing habits!"

"Please, Cat, I am not in the mood for lectures." Pup said with tears in his eyes.

"Guess not, Pup. I am actually sad that you will be gone." Cat said placing her arm around Pup's shoulder.

Pup replied, "Only because you need me to open the food bag for midnight snacks!"

"Although, it pierces my heart to admit this, I have grown fond of you in a certain kind of way and yes, I'll miss your assistance in the food opening process." Cat said as Pup hugged her tight.

"Sorry I didn't take your advice, Cat."

"Well, let this be a lesson to you in your new home. No chewing up the place, you inferior fur ball!"

Floyd was even sad to see Pup leave, "Oh boy, Oh boy, good-bye Pup!" he could be heard saying.

While all the fur balls were saying their good-byes, a thief came through the window. He was stealing Mom's silverware when Pup starting barking. The thief tried to push Pup away to keep him quiet, but not before Pup bit his pant leg holding him down until Mom and George came running downstairs.

"Good Pup! Hold him down, boy!" George said as Mom called the police.

Pup, was on the TV news and given the title, HERO! He protected his family and he was now allowed to stay with George.

"If it weren't for Pup being there, who knows what could have happened! I don't care what he chews up from now on! Pup will always have a home with us!" Dad said.

Once the story spread about Pup's heroic act, everyone wanted to see the hero dog.

Puppies Dog Food Company asked George if Pup wanted to do TV commercials.

"It's up to Pup if he wants to be on TV. Either way, we love him and he is our hero!"

Pup became a big TV star and sold lots of dog food. George donated the money to the animal shelters to help others. Whenever George took Pup out for a walk, he was always recognized as the hero dog. Pup's life couldn't have been better until one day when the Evil Diva showed up. She claimed that she lost Pup and came to take him back.

"Pup is your dog?" George asked.

"Yes. He somehow got... lost." Evil Diva said.

"How can we be sure he is yours?" Mom asked.

Evil Diva gave Dad the paperwork she had as proof that Pup was hers. Mom, Dad and George tried to convince her to leave Pup with them but all she cared about was the money.

"We will give you every penny Pup makes from the commercials, but please don't take him away!" Dad said.

"Please, lady, don't take my Pup away!" George said holding onto Pup.

"We are willing to even pay you any amount for Pup!" Mom said.

"You couldn't afford to pay me enough compared to what I will make off of him! He was a useless chewing troublemaker before I kicked him out..."

"You KICKED him out? You said you LOST him! Please, Dad, do something!" George yelled out.

"Please, let him stay..." Dad tried but Evil Diva had made up her mind.

"NO, he is mine and I want him back! The TV commercial money is a joke! I will make even more once I sell him to the movie studios!" Evil Diva said as she tried to drag Pup to the front door.

"You are a very evil woman!" Dad said.

"Yes, I have been told that and frankly, I don't care! Now come on, you once good-for-nothing animal!" Evil Diva said as she picked up Pup and left.

As each day passed, George missed Pup and wondered how he was doing. Mom and Dad noticed that Pup wasn't in the TV commercials any longer. And they also noticed that George was still very sad. They offered to get George another dog but he didn't want any other dog except Pup.

"I don't understand why there are evil people and why God allows evil." George said.

Mom and Dad didn't have all the answers but they did try to explain to George about evil.

"God allows things to happen for reasons that we can't understand. But He always has a plan and we have to trust that He is doing what is best for us."

"I still don't see it that way. That evil woman took our dog away and didn't really love him as we did. Doesn't God see that?" George asked.

"God sees everything, George, even what is going to happen in the future," Dad said.

"Does he see how much I miss Pup?"

"Yes, and He sees more than that. God does not always remove us from all harm. He uses harm to move us closer to Him. He allowed this to happen but in the end, there will be a lesson to be learned." Mom added.

"And when you believe that God is good no matter what, that lesson will be shown to you." Dad said.

George tried to understand but his true feelings came out, "I hate Evil Diva!"

"George, no matter how evil that woman is, you should never have hate in your heart. The Bible says, 'Do this and you will overcome evil with good. Let love be genuine.' Love her instead of hating her. It's what God would want you to do. Can you trust that God is in control, even when evil strikes?" Mom asked.

"Yes, I will try, Mom." George said hoping he could keep his word.

Some time went by and then one day, there was a knock on the door followed by a bark.

"That sounds like Pup!" George said running to open the door.

Standing there on the front porch was Pup! And along with him was Evil Diva.

"Pup it's really you! I missed you so much!" George said as Pup jumped up on him.

"You can have the worthless pup back. He wouldn't do anything in front of the TV cameras for me!" Evil Diva said as she started to leave.

George ran to Evil Diva, "Wait, wait please! I'm sorry Pup didn't do what you wanted him to do and I'm sorry I was so mad at you, but I'm not...mad at you anymore. God showed me how to overcome evil with good by loving you instead of hating you. I trusted in Him and now understand why evil has to happen at times. I forgive you."

"Do you really forgive me?" Evil Diva asked looking surprised.

"Yes, of course!" George answered.

With tears in her eyes, Evil Diva apologized for what she did and told George that she really didn't want to be evil anymore.

Mom and Dad welcomed Pup home and then invited Evil Diva to come in for dinner. George hugged Pup and said, "I love you, Pup!"

"Oh brother...he's back! But I love him too!" Cat said.

The End

Luke 6:27-28:

But to you who are listening,
I say: Love your enemies, do good to those who hate you,
bless those who curse you, pray for those who mistreat you.